WINTER'S L

A romanticised moorland drama set in late 18th to
early 19th century Devon, England.
A peasant family are driven to risk all,
in a life-or-death struggle.
By
Kelia-Jane Hannah

KJH

Published by
Goodness Me Publishing Limited
www.goodnessmepublishing.co.uk

Cover design and illustrations
by
Devon based artist, Kim Moody.
(Additional photos by KJH)

Text copyright © 2021

Dedication –To all those, willing to face the greatest of
odds with courage and fortitude,
and never give up.

'Our mistakes hurt us most,
when it is we, that finally discover them.'

KJH

"There comes a point on your journey, that regardless of the
difficulties, it becomes less arduous to continue,
than it is to go back."
"Pride should be tempered with practicality, and shame
belongs not in failure, but in not doing your best."

If you have ever walked the moors in snow, mist, or
darkness, then you will know exactly what I mean.

The one we can truly trust most, is ourselves.
Sometimes that is simply not enough.
KJH

Modern times and an old tale :-

It is 6th of March 2021, we are in a partly modernised farmhouse on the wild moors of the Exe, several miles Northwest of the small village of Challacombe. The house had been up for sale many a long month. Its remote location and the spectre of ghosts, dissuading potential new owners, but today . . . success.

Fingering the keys to his modern Range Rover in his pocket, the estate agent smiled with satisfaction upon the proud new buyers of Ashcombe Oak Farm, 'I just know you'll love this place, especially when you expressed excitement about buying a remote property with a ghost. The previous owners didn't mind either; they told me it's a kindly ghost, possibly that of an old shepherd, recorded as missing, presumed lost on the moors.   Quaintly, it knocks on the door of the original part of the farmhouse when it snows. Isn't that lovely? When they opened the door there was nobody there and no footprints in the snow either. People love these old wives' tales, makes the moors more romantic, more interesting, don't you think? Still, we rarely have much snow here nowadays.

'Oh! I forgot to tell you, when the previous owners added the new extension, they had to lift some cobbles, and guess what?

4

They found a golden guinea dated 1779, most probably lost by some careless rich bloke. Perhaps there's more out there. . . here's hoping for you eh?'

**

The story of winter's longest sleep: - Please, come and sit awhile with us, as I share this incredible tale of endurance, strength and courage. Courage likely beyond our understanding in this modern age. Feel the family love that survives in eternity, witness the loyalty, trust, sadness and loss, and meet the heroes of our tale in their encounter with the natural cycle of life and death, so stoically accepted by those who have lived upon the moors.

It is easy for us to glibly judge in the rose-tinted spectacles of hindsight the choices made at the time. Ask yourself, in the face of starvation and betrayal, would you really have acted any differently?

Tell me at the end.

**

Comfortable? Then we'll begin:-

The date is 1786 and like many peasants of the day, George Dinnicombe was yet another hard-working victim of the social order of the age, often surviving on subsistence wages in return for risking his all, his life, his family and his soul. Slavery in all but name. He was ever eager for the opportunity to provide for his family.

George was born to poverty-stricken parents in the winter of 1752, and, when old enough to work, was given away and bound to a Thomas Reid, owner of a blacksmith and farriery business not far from the Devon village of Loxhore.

George did well as apprentice to Thomas Reid, a kindly and likeable gentleman with an excellent reputation for anything to do with horses and ironwork. George proved himself over again as a willing worker and a keen learner, and soon became indispensable to the Reid's family business. His life was as good as could be expected for a working man. In 1774, age twenty-two, George, a fine looking, strong young man, had married Phoebe. Phoebe Goulde was a God fearing and kind-hearted young lass from the nearby village of Stoke Rivers. She also came from an impoverished family; her father having succumbed to Smallpox the year before she reached twenty and married George at St Bartholomew in her own parish. The couple were blessed with three children, all healthy and strong - William 11, Thomas 9, and their endearing sister Sarah 6.

Old Mr Reid, the owner of the business, had two sons, Mark, and a younger rival sibling, Luke, of whom it must be fairly said was nothing but a downright wastrel and a most disappointing son for the decent minded and kindly Thomas Reid.

It was a bad day for all, when the good Thomas Reid was finally laid to rest. Thomas' funeral was a fine affair and well attended by the local community, in particular by the many that were in his debt for past favours. None were surprised by the absence of the spendthrift Luke, who had ridden into Barnstaple town to celebrate his inheritance in the only way he knew. Subsequently, his careless drinking and gambling incurred increasing debts upon the business, and despite Mark Reid's best efforts they soon had to let workers go - A still popular euphemism for terminating employment and evicting loyal and trusty servants of many years.

On the third of March 1786 it was George's turn, he was the last to go. The business had failed completely by then, due to Luke's so called 'friends' calling in their markers.

Mark Reid retained a small cottage from the estate, in which he continued to live with his grieving mother. None of their employees could be afforded such luxuries, nor did they expect such. None of these events were going to be easy for anyone. By the dying heat of the forge, George and Mark stood in solemnity, already aware of the other's mind, 'I'm deeply sorry George. We've grown up together here and I had great hopes we would all grow old in dignity and peace together too. It's not to be. The cottage you live in is no longer mine to control. You will have to move out, I'm profoundly sorry. I can tell you how bad it is, the horses we have, those few that are left, I cannot even afford to feed. I'm not sure how I will survive but am hopeful one of my father's acquaintances may take pity on me and find me a position.'

'I'm sorry too sir for your loss, don't you worry about us sir, I shall think of something. . . don't you worry sir. I shall go and speak with Phoebe, and we'll make our plans,' said George with a confidence in his voice that belied his sense of immense loss. Mark had been like a brother all these years, and old Mr Reid had been like a kindly uncle to him all through his education and service.

It wasn't the first time George had struggled alone and he didn't suppose it would be the last either. As he walked away from the smithy, across the once weed free, inner cobbled yard and under the barn to the lane outside, he met Luke coming the other way. As usual he was the worse for drink but treated George with the respect bullies often have for those who are in nature and in stature their betters, 'Sorry to see you go George old chap, you're a fine fellow, good-looking wife too I'll say.'

Something in the back of his mind inspired George to ask a favour, 'Luke, sir, if you cannot feed the horses, could you see your way to let me have one in payment for all the times I saved you from your troubles in the past?'

'George old chap, help yourself, no, tell you what, I'll pick one out myself and tether her outside the barn for you. That big bay with the black mane is a fine horse. You leave it with me. You can trust me not to let you down.' With that, he staggered off to confront his susceptibly naive brother over some trifling amount but which he still desperately needed.

George walked thoughtfully to the comparative hovel they called a cottage, which nevertheless was a home of happy times, a daring plan taking shape in his mind. At the back of the cottage was a rundown open farm cart in need of better rims and some other attention, what with that fine horse Luke had promised and a few running repairs to the cart they could use it to start a new life where there was more work. Many a traveller seeking the farrier at the smithy had shared their tales of riches and fine living in towns such as Bristol. Riches fostered by the ships that sailed to and from the new world. This was a bold but fine plan.

Phoebe listened in silence as he broke the news. She thought a while, then said quietly, 'Why George dear, could they not tell you last week when you would have had a chance of work at the hiring fair. You are a good man with fine skills, you would have found work to be sure. . . and it is three months to the next one. . . and us now homeless with winter not yet past. That Luke will surely go to hell, for certain he should. I pity his poor mother, God bless her.'

The children, though not fully understanding the implications, had heard the news. They had such faith in their father, they were not afraid, it seemed like an adventure.

'We will leave tomorrow morning. While I prepare the cart, you must gather together what little we have. There may be a few root vegetables still good enough to lift. . . William, you can do that. Otherwise just help your mother in whatever she asks. While there is daylight left I will begin on the old cart,' and so saying, he was gone to the rear of the cottage, tools in hand.

That night they all had a good supper and kept the fire well banked, no point in leaving firewood for the next tenant. Nobody slept well that night, their minds in turmoil over the great unknown that awaited them.

As a pale grey March dawn approached slowly from the east, bringing with it a cold wind off the moors, George was already preparing to leave. He had on his working clothes and thick coat, as his old boots clumped up the stony lane for one last time to the stables. He was in for a dreadful shock. No fine bay horse awaited him, just an old nag of twenty years or more. The poor animal was more suited to feeding the hounds at his Lordship's hunt than pull a cart.

George was staring at the old grey mare in a mixture of disbelief, sorrow and surprise, when Mark's voice startled him from the barn doorway. 'George, George, my dear friend, I am so sorry this has happened. Luke was angry I had no more money for him yesterday, so he took all the horses, leaving only old Molly here. He said she probably wouldn't reach town alive anyway. It's all there is my friend, all there is and nothing anymore to be done about it.'

'Never you mind sir, not your doing, we'll care for her, make the best of it as we always have,' George assured, as he released the tether to walk Molly down to the cottage.

Mark held out his hand, George took it and the warmth of fellowship flowed in their veins. As Mark released his grip, George looked in his hand. . . a golden Guinea looked back at him. 'No need to say anything George, take it for any emergency you might face. It's all I have; I wish it were more, for you were ever a better brother to me than that prodigal drunkard with whom I have the misfortune to share parents. I wish you all well and tell you, most sincerely, I will never forget you and your loyal service to my father. Goodbye George.'

Outside their humble cottage, Phoebe looked in astonishment at the old horse, but young Sarah instantly loved the quiet gentleness of the aging grey. They'd never had a horse before.

'I know, I know,' agreed George, 'I know she's old, but if we are careful and do our fair share of walking, we'll survive. If we stay here we'll starve or freeze for sure. We must always make the best of what we have. Come on boys, you can help me harness her in the shafts.'

KJH

Their adventure to a new freedom was beginning. Most roads in those days were extremely poor, almost impassable in places. It became fashionable for the rich to improve the more important roads and charge people for using them. George chose instead to take isolated and remote moorland tracks as it would be many miles shorter, it avoided the levies of toll roads and there would be free grazing for the family's new horse. Exmoor was renowned for being remote, sparsely populated, and often served only by pack horse trails.

It all began well, with the children and Phoebe walking alongside, George leading the horse, encouraging with kind words gleaned from so many years of his trade. After a few miles they left the small tree-filled combes behind and started the steady climb on to the wilds of Exmoor. They stopped only briefly near mid-day, for daylight was still precious in the month of March. The pace was slow and entirely dependent on Molly the horse. Each hour would only see them another painstaking and weary two miles along the ancient tracks of the moor.

Then, George smiled and looked back at his despondently trudging family, 'Look! Look there, lady luck is smiling upon us.' He pointed to a small but well-situated farmstead ahead and down to his right. It was only a gentle slope to the farm, it looked a touch run down but had all the essentials, running water, sheltered valley, small orchard, a good number of trees for fuel and even a low-lying pasture field that could be cultivated. Sarah ambled alongside and chatted to her newfound childhood friend, Molly the grey horse, who walked slowly on at the perfect pace for the charming six-year-old. George waved an open hand back to the farmer, who had been struggling with a broken fence. They greeted each other warmly, one for the comfort of shelter and the other the comfort of company.

The farmer introduced himself as William Beer and as he did so, a pleasantly smiling plump lady wiping her hands on a cloth appeared at the open farmhouse door, 'and this is my good wife, Sarah.' And then, after hearing the traveller's story, William Beer insisted, 'You shall dine with us tonight and the barn is sound enough for shelter. . . it looks like your old horse could do with a rest. . . a long rest!' They all laughed, forgetting all their troubles in that brief moment of joy.

The coincidence of two Williams and two Sarahs was not lost on them, it created an impression of kinship, as in those days children were often named after their grandparents. Old Sarah made a fine fuss of young Sarah and the boys sat by the inglenook fire with their mother.

George, having seen the needy state of the farm, offered a day's work from him and the boys in return for the hospitality.

'Gladly accepted George my friend, gladly indeed. Sadly, we were not blessed with any children that God made strong enough to survive their first years. We're getting older now and yesterday I strained my shoulder trying to keep a wayward ewe from jumping that cursed broken fence you saw me struggling with. Sarah's not up to lifting heavy things either!' Old William smiled a knowing smile.

In the two days the Dinnicombe family finally stayed at the farm, situated not so many miles north of Challacombe, they transformed the place, fences mended, wood collected, chopped, and stacked, barn hinges straightened and replaced, weeds cut, water fetched, roof patched. It was a hive of activity, a gloriously happy occasion, but then it was time to leave, for George was drawn to a different future.

The morning of their departure, old William the farmer, with his wife close by, spoke quietly and earnestly to George, 'George, you can see the future this farm holds for someone younger, we have no living relatives, no children to take over when we are gone. We would like to offer your boy William a home with us, treat him kindly like one of our own and one day he will become the farmer here.' Old Sarah clasped her hands together in prayerful hope, Phoebe's hidden hand pinched her husband's arm.

George understood the situation well enough, however, due to his own traumatic childhood experiences, George had already decided what he needed to do, the family must all stay together.

'In my heart I cannot countenance such a thing, though I see the kindness of your offer and feel for your loss as if it were my very own. We must move on and leave you with happy memories and a knowing that you will always be remembered. But for now, our destiny lies elsewhere.'

As they gathered at the farm gate, preparing to leave and say their farewells, old William warned George of bad weather to come, 'Winter's not over yet George, the wind from the East and the colour of the morning's sunrise tells me that it's possible we may have snow. . . the moor is no place for anyone when that happens. You are always welcome back here if it proves to be too hard going.'

Their handshake was deep in the meaning of lasting kinship.

'Don't worry, William, we shall be fine, two days at most and we'll be off the moor and on the sheltered wooded lowlands,' assured a confident George, a most capable man in his mid-thirties and with abundant strength and energy.

They walked with the horse to the top of the slope, only young Sarah hitching a ride on the back, waving her many last goodbyes to the dear old lady who'd been like the grandmother she never knew.

William and Sarah Beer stood together as they always had and waved until the cart and all were gone from sight, though not from mind. They walked slowly back to their house; their hearts filled with the dreams of what might have been.

The old drover's track was still passably visible and in general followed either the contour lines or the ridges. They were making reasonable time until nature hindered their path. A small but unavoidable valley. Evident, from the reed growth and sphagnum moss that spread some twenty yards or so across the valley bottom, it was the sort of boggy challenge they could well have done without.

'Everybody off the cart, even you Sarah, lift off some of the heavy things and we'll come back for them,' George was still confident it could be done, but oh for a stronger, younger horse. It was almost as much as Molly could do to lift her feet out of the bog, never mind pull the cart, which had only made her hooves sink deeper. 'Come on boys, hands to the wheel spokes, and you too Phoebe,' called George enthusiastically as he heaved at the harness and encouraged Molly to do her best. She was a willing horse and needed no flogging. The wheels wobbled side to side with their worn bearings and rocked back and forth as the cart teetered on leaving a deep rut. With rests, it must have taken the family a good half an hour to place the cart on firm ground again. It was painfully obvious that Molly was now lame. Experience told George it was probably a tendon in the lower leg, the swelling had already started, she might be able to hobble on for a while but pulling the cart would probably kill her. It wouldn't be the first horse he'd seen broken winded with age and excessive labour. There was little shelter in the valley of mostly grass and winter-dead bracken, though it was less windy than on the tops where the east wind was beginning to carry sleet. The sky was turning the peculiar grey that brought the smell of snow.

'Right Phoebe, we must be a good seven or so miles from the Beer's farm, perhaps over the ridge there may be another. Shelter as best you can in the cart, I'll be as quick as I can to fetch help.'

Phoebe noticed the change in George's voice, she knew he was worried, she knew that they should have heeded old William's warning and now their very lives were in God's hands. Sleet began to fall more heavily as George slowly clambered from sight, collar up and leaning into both hill and strengthening wind that now conspired so cruelly against him. Phoebe prepared the contents of the cart as best she could to make a shelter, she leaned against the woodworm riddled side and gathered her children close, Sarah on her lap and the boys each side, pieces of sack cloth and a sheet of old darned canvas their only protection from the east wind's determined onslaught. The cold, hunting wind howled through gaps in the cart's sides and the torn canvas flapped noisily about them.

Phoebe knew only too well the truth of the matter, not all of them would live through this storm. None the less, she reassured the children that all would be well, that their father would not let them down and would never leave them alone on the moor. She knew in her heart of hearts he would always come back, whatever barred his way.

Molly, now free from her traces and left untethered, stood resolute with her back to the biting wind and the sleet that slowly changed her grey to white. There was only one thing she was waiting for, and it didn't disappoint. It wasn't long before she fell quietly to the ground, unnoticed, her work was over.

George reached the summit with failing visibility but sufficient for him to view the surrounding empty moor. In front was another small valley, it shouldn't take him long to cross it and see if here was a farm the other side, or perhaps a shelter wood. He pushed himself harder than ever, his feet numbingly cold through the worn-thin soles of his boots, and his hands were pained by the touch of cold wet sleet, a pain much like burning from the forge, his hands had lost so much feeling he could no longer close a button nor adjust his collar. There were moments when he wondered if he should have turned back, but any doubt was quickly extinguished by the mindless fear deep within him that drove his stumbling legs still further into the blizzard. He knew as well as Phoebe, that they would not all survive this storm, but he was not dead yet and he must find help for his family. 'Just one more hill,' he promised himself, and with fading hope and strength, 'just one more hill.'

Meanwhile the sleet had turned to snow, big snowflakes riding the wind towards him faster than galloping horses, almost pretty to watch, practically mesmerising. . . George shook his head from this strange but passing fascination and pressed on.

In the meantime, back at the cart, Phoebe's mind was in turmoil, what if George did not come back in time, even if he did, will they still be strong enough to move? She thought about Mr. Beer's generous offer to care for her eldest boy William. Possibly seven miles back to the farm it was, but young William was a strong boy, well-nourished and big for his age, he had the determination of his father and the spirit of his mother.

She made her decision.

Daylight would not last forever, maybe four or five hours at most left, if William started out now, while he was still able, with the wind at his back and before the snow deepened further, he could make a dogged one-way hike to the farm before nightfall. Phoebe gently lifted Sarah, who appeared to be sleeping quietly now, to one side, she took off her coat and made William put it on, she wrapped him up well and asked him, 'Tell me William, do you think you can follow the way back to the farm?' William was subdued but nodded back in reply. 'Then off you go with my blessing, may God be with you and guide you all the way safe to the Beer's farm,' she kissed his cold forehead, pulled his cap down tight and helped him off the cart. 'Don't you stop,' she said, 'if you get tired you do not stop, you keep going, say hello to them and we send our love.'

'Don't you stop William. . . whatever happens, you keep going!' she shouted after him.

William turned, nodded again, and was gone in an instant, he felt very grown up that his mother entrusted him with such a journey. . . he would not fail her.

Sheltered by two coats, with the cold wind at his back blowing the snow past him, his path was clearer, his body warmer and his intention resolute.

Phoebe had settled back in the cart as best she could, already her precious Sarah the youngest was sleeping the long sleep, Thomas huddled ever closer, his shivering body telling Phoebe he was still alive. She pulled the canvas and sacking tight around their bodies and quietly prayed, first for Sarah, then for William, Thomas and for her brave George wherever he was, and only then for herself.

George's mind was confused, he was still walking but no longer sure in which direction, for snow had already covered the ground and filled his footprints. He'd long since stopped shivering and was so tired he desperately wanted to rest. Then astonishingly, through the curtain of snow, like an apparition, came another man walking towards him. The other spoke and beckoned him on. Though George could not hear above the wind, bemused, he followed the stranger to a small cob-built shepherd's shelter, it had a simple but adequate heather thatched roof, and best of all a small fire of Gorse wood burned at one end. The host explained that he was a local shepherd looking for lost sheep before the blizzard took its icy grip upon the moor.

George, not able to recognize his rapidly worsening hypothermia, spoke in a slurred voice, hardly recognising it as his own, and begged about his family needing help. The shepherd told him of a small farm two miles further east, just off the ridge-way track. Though pleased with such news, George again felt extraordinarily drowsy. He took off his big coat to warm it by the fire and promised himself just a few minutes rest before pressing on to the farm. Just a few minutes, that's all, it wouldn't hurt. In a moment he fell fast asleep, it never occurred to him that even if he reached the farm he was still lost, he would never find the cart again in this storm.

It was in that precise fateful moment that Phoebe stopped praying for his return. Hope and breath lay themselves peacefully down in the snow with the old grey horse, all victims to the worsening storm.

George woke keenly, his eyes instantly acclimatised to the dazzling whiteness about him. Feeling refreshed and comforted, with what he assumed had been only moments of rest, he glanced about him to see the shepherd had gone and the cob walls of the shelter were just snow-covered remnants. George set off with renewed determination towards the farm the shepherd had described to him, his mind not in any state to question the events of his journey. He reached the farm with seemingly little effort, his hands no longer burned with the pain of cold, his footsteps were light and easy. He reached into his pocket for the one gold coin he had, the guinea that Mark had given him. He would use it to buy help for his family. His closed fist knocked heavily on the solid farmhouse door, but it remained closed. Twice more he beat on the door and called out in anguish for someone to come. In the muffled silence of falling snow, the door remained steadfastly deaf to his desperate pleas. He could stay no longer, something dear to his soul was calling to him from across the moors. He turned and ran westwards, quickly blending into the deepening and all-pervading whiteness. He would never give up, all that mattered to him was out there, lost somewhere on a moor that more often than not, buried its secrets. A terrible sense of loss had grabbed hold of his spirit, in this instant, George knew he must search forever.

As winter followed winter, George's ghost, condemned to remain the still valiant young man in his thirties, would search the snow bound moors, on occasion chancing across the lost shepherd, who in dutiful eternity still sought his sheep.

**

The Beer's Farmstead 1786

You might well ask, 'what of the young boy William?'

Alone and lost in the cruel grip of a blizzard, could this mere child possibly find the strength of body and mind to fight his way back across the moor to the Beer's farm?

We can only trust and hope, as did his loving mother when she sent him on his way. They all faced an unknown, and each would meet it in their own way.

KJH

Many years have come and gone, and we now find ourselves at the Beer's farm in the month of March, during the year of our lord, 1809. On the continent, Napoleonic wars impose misery upon country after country, creating shortages of manpower and food in England.

William, now thirty-four, is the same age as his father had been when he was lost to the great snowstorm back in 1786. The same fateful day when William himself was saved by his mother's ultimate and breath-taking sacrifice. We re-join William at the Beer's old farm, 1809, another cold day in March.

Even before dawn had broken, William had sensed snow was approaching in the east wind, and he had tirelessly busied himself all day about the farm, ensuring the livestock were safely sheltered, hay was in place, roots were dug, firewood collected, and fences checked.

As the first candle flame of the evening fluttered gamely in a draught by the low casement window, William rested his tired body in a seat by the inglenook, the farm dog at his feet enjoying a treat by the fire. He began to reflect deeply on his dear wife Hannah and on their three children who were now growing up so fast. He speculated about finding a decent apprenticeship for the oldest boy, Thomas, now eleven, and named after both Hannah's father and William's own brother. Thomas was the same age as William had been when he had fought his way back through that great storm that caused such heartbreak, exactly twenty-three years ago to the day.

KJH

He watched, fascinated, as falling snow filled the small panes in the window frame ... his eyes closed gently... he remembered his father and the storm on the moor, like it was only yesterday . . . .

His mother, Phoebe, and the three children were trapped in a deadly blizzard high up on the moors. His father, George, a confident and powerful man, had pressed on into the storm, hoping to find a nearby farm and help. Their old and ailing horse Molly had drawn its last breath. The worm riddled sides of the cart and an old, tattered canvas their only shelter.

Phoebe had carefully reconsidered farmer Beer's earlier generous offer to care for her eldest boy. Young William at eleven was a strong boy, with the determination of his father and the spirit of his mother. She had made her decision, the most difficult of her life. Daylight would not last forever, maybe four or five hours left at best to cover the six or seven miles. If William started out while he was still strong enough, with the wind at his back and before the snow deepened, he could reach the farm before nightfall.

Phoebe had gently lifted Sarah, who appeared to be sleeping quietly, to one side, then she took off her coat and made William put it on, she wrapped him up well and asked him, 'Tell me William, can you find your way back to the farm?' William nodded back in reply. 'Then off you go with my blessing, may God be with you and guide you all the way, safe to the Beer's farm.'

She kissed his cold forehead, pulled his cap down tight and helped him off the cart. 'Don't you stop,' she said, 'if you are tired you do not stop, you keep going, say hello to them and that we send our love. Don't you stop William. . . whatever happens, you must never stop!' she shouted after him.

William turned, nodded again, and was gone in an instant. . . he would not fail her.

Sheltered by two coats, with the snow blowing past him as if pointing the way, his path was clearer, his body warmer and his intention resolute.

Driven on, in part by fear, in part by the promise to his mother, and in part, with the childish notion that the Beers would quickly organise a rescue and save his mother and family from the storm, William found the track relatively easy to see as it followed the contours of the hills. With the wind pushing him along, his progress was quick, though with no gloves, his hands were painfully cold, his fingers had soon lost their ability to close, he pushed each hand into the opposite sleeve of his mother's coat and strode on. Once, a huge snow drift hindered his way, he turned to look back, wondering if he should return to his mother, but the snow blinded his eyes and the east wind ripped like a jagged knife at his face. Right away he knew for sure there was only one direction to take, and now, even more determined not to let anything stop him, he bypassed the drift and strode on with renewed vigour. It seemed as though he had been walking forever, and finding the Beer's farm, seemed nigh on impossible, when suddenly he smelled wood smoke in the air. He had unwittingly passed by the slope down to the farm a short way back. The smell of smoke on the east wind gave him renewed strength and it was with excitement, forgetting all else, that he ran the last few yards to the farm door. Despite his urgent quest, he was still respectful enough to knock.

The door was soon opened, William and Sarah Beer were thrilled to see him, though they had fully expected the family to return not long after the snow had begun to fall. The old couple looked past William, peering into the storm and fast falling dusk, eagerly looking for the rest of the family. Their expressions asked the question and William simply answered, 'I'm alone, mother sent me back. She sends her love.'

The old couple pulled William safely inside, closed the door to the cruel world beyond, and gave him warm soup and a blanket. His hands fumbled to hold the spoon and his lips were numb with cold. As the burning pain in his hands slowly subsided, William realised that this dear old couple were in no fit state to carry out any rescue. It was not long after, that exhaustion and exposure took their toll and the poor boy succumbed to a deep and protective sleep.

Next day and for three days after, his body ached all over from his struggle to survive on the moor. Old William Beer, his wife standing behind him with her comforting hands gently on his shoulders, called young William over to sit at the table and spoke solemnly to him. 'My boy, we must all of us face the facts, this is how life is and sometimes how it ends, we none of us can escape this. The snow is deeper now and the track impossible to follow. No one could survive out there, we must be grateful that you are here.'

Old William could see the spirit ebbing out of young William as his loss fell heavily upon him.

With his voice calm but earnest, he continued, 'Young William, my dearest boy, hear this and hear it well, your mother gave you life, in fact she handed you that most treasured of gifts not once, but twice. Now it is up to you to fulfil all she wanted for you. Now is your time to stand tall and honour her wish that you be chosen to live on and to do well. Be strong, remember them as they were in happy times and live the life you were gifted to the full. Sarah and I will help you all we can. Time will be a great healer, you will see.'

Young William was shielded from the recovery of the family's bodies, carried out a week or so later by villagers and farmers near to the moor.

Simple coffins were laid to rest in a patch of sloping ground at the back of the farm, where the graves of earlier Beers also overlooked the track and gateway to the copse past the stream. The burial was a solemn and poignant occasion, followed by a hearty meal in the farmhouse for all those attending. Somehow, the warmth of good company and shared food made for an unexpected happy occasion. It was the beginning of a new era. William's father was never found, and it left him with a burning question that might well take a lifetime to answer.

Old William and Sarah Beer were as good as their word, she loved him like the son she had always wanted, and he taught the boy all he knew about farming and life on the moors, he shared all the secret ways and wisdoms passed down through the ages. There was the planting of kale and potatoes, mangel beet for the livestock, leeks, onions, and other vegetables. Harvesting and thrashing the small barley crop, lambing, and fleecing, watching the pigs among the oak and beech trees at the right time of year. Storing the barley straw, picking fruit at harvest time, securing the ducks, geese, and chickens from the moorland fox, and so many other labour-intensive jobs. Young William, like his father before him, worked hard, learned well, and had a respectful yet affable attitude to others. He grew from strength to strength, and it seemed there was nothing he could not do.

He was home where he was loved and valued.

The dog, stood, stretched, and lay down again by the fire and in so doing, brushed against William's feet. He partially woke from his dream, just long enough to hear Hannah tell George and Thomas to go to sleep, their six-year-old sister Sarah, already peacefully in her own land of dreams. Hearing Hannah's voice pleased William greatly and he settled himself comfortably again in his seat and remembered their first meeting.

Oh, they were good days back then, he was about sixteen, able to deal rationally with his past sorrows and had steadfastly gained old William Beer's respect. 'Find your coat young William and harness the horse to the small cart. I'm taking you to a horse fair.'

Though he was excited enough by that, it was nothing compared to what was to happen later that day. They made their way with much admired skill over almost trackless moor and down the valley towards Challacomb.

'Stay by me lad at the fair, and best not speak unless I ask,' advised the wily old farmer, 'we need to drive a good bargain, hill farming will never make us rich. My dear old horse has served me well but might only have another good year in her. We must find a fitting replacement today. Something suitable for a light plough and small cart would suit us fine.'

The village was packed full of people from many miles around, some to sell, some to buy, others for the spectacle and thrill. The horse fair was only held once a year. Now, old William had a good friend there, Joseph Goulde, the village blacksmith and farrier, and it was to him they went first to hear the local gossip on bargains to be had. Young William did as he was asked and stood quietly and close by the man he had come to treat as his father.

The smells and the heat of the forge though, brought memories flooding back of happy days with his late family, but he had long accepted it was time to move on and he was now often referred to as young William Beer.

Peacefully walking along the busy village road, they were suddenly confronted by a commotion in front. A pretty girl about William's age, with flowing auburn hair over her shoulders and carrying a basket full of eggs for sale, was being accosted by a much older man. A stooping man of slender build, wearing expensive clothes that had long since seen their best days.

A shocked hush fell swiftly over the watching crowd as old William abruptly and roughly jarred his stick into the man's chest, stopping him instantly in his tracks. The girl demonstrated her gratitude with a smile of recognition and the man showed his resentment and contempt with a sneer and a threat. A threat that came to nothing as the villain caught the look on young William's face, a look that spoke of untold strength and determination, a look reminiscent of someone else he had once admired and yet also feared. As young William moved shoulder to shoulder with old William, he did so with a new admiration for this old man's courage. Meanwhile, the evil villain of the piece, slunk away into the crowd, muttering. The young lady gave a little curtsey, thanked Mr. Beer by name and with a swish of her russet dress and holding her basket in both hands, walked away. Young William felt the ache as his heart was captured and carried away by the young lady.

Even more so, when after just a few steps, she turned her head, tilted it to one side and smiled straight at him. A smile that would abide forever within his soul.

Seeing that William was somewhat curious about events, old William explained. 'That man is an evil waster, well known for his drinking and gambling. He's been the utter ruin of many good folk across Exmoor. Luke Reid is his name – avoid him lad – he's always trouble.'

Old William left a suitably lengthy and poignant pause, then with a knowing grin continued, 'Oh, if you must know, the young lady is Hannah, Joe Richards' daughter. He runs a small farm not so distant from ours but not as high up the moor. We can call there on the way home, show him our new mare, once we've bought one of course. In fact, we can offer Hannah a lift home.' From that day on, there was only one person on Earth for William – the lovely Hannah Richards.

Old William Beer chuckled to himself; it was more than a horse he'd be taking home. His wife would be thrilled with the gossip.

The trip back to the farm with their newly acquired and freshly shod three-year-old horse, did not transpire quite as William had hoped. Yes, they gave Hannah a lift, and her older brother too. Hannah sat up front with old William Beer, chatting amicably about all manner of things, while the two young men shared the back of the cart. An occasional laugh from the merry pair at the front embarrassed the self-conscious young William into thinking that he might be part of the joke. They later spent about half an hour engaging with the Richards' family, though young William remained unusually quiet. Whenever he could, he watched Hannah, who, catching his glances, blushed and hid her face. The two young people hid their attraction for each other, even though it was amusingly obvious to everyone else. Old William Beer arranged some shared labour for harvest and shearing times. Both he and Thomas Richards were getting older, and it was time for the younger men to take over the heavier duties. They left the Richards' farm for home in good spirits, though over the next few days, Sarah Beer good naturedly amused herself with young William's loss of appetite ... 'was he ill?' she enquired with a smile.

Over the months, William did manage to see Hannah a few times, though it was always during a working visit, for farming on the edge of the moors paid scant attention to the niceties of socialising for pleasure. A situation that could have proved intolerable was all made good when young William, now a fine young man with prospects, realised that Hannah felt just the same way about him. It was obvious to them both, for when they saw each other, the world was suddenly a better place, they felt complete.

Two years later, and when William had looked forward so much to seeing Hannah at the horse fair, she was missing. He'd looked and looked but there was no sign of her. They met one of her brothers, 'Hannah? She's been sent away to stay with an ailing aunt, to look after her until she gets better. No idea how long, we don't need her at the farm anyway . . .'

It was like a horse had kicked him in the chest, he felt sick and was poor company for old William as they made their way home. The farm work kept him busy, and his previous losses had taught him that things can always get better. Though they were indeed to appear worse in the months ahead. Another year had passed, and Sarah Beer fell ill, she took to her bed and showed no sign of recovery.

Life became difficult for the two men, more difficult than ever before. A farmer's wife was never idle, storing of fruit, making cider, butter, and cheese, collecting eggs, combing and spinning wool, pickling pork, smoking and salting meat, keeping house, darning and mending, and feeding the men, now this also fell upon the menfolk of the farm, and they were struggling badly. The doctor had visited and thought it something akin to typhus, but unlikely, with no other cases about. Sarah Beer deteriorated, young William felt the pain of not only his own loss but that of old William, a dear kind and devoted man if ever there was.

One early autumn morning, a cart drew into the yard, it was Mrs. Richards come to help, and joy of joys, she had brought Hannah with her. There was little could be done for Sarah Beer except to comfort her until a peaceful end came. However, it had meant the men could return to essential prewinter farm labours and be fed properly as well. Sitting at the table with a fine warming soup, William looked lovingly across at Hannah as she stood by an embers fire in the inglenook, the glow of setting sunlight shone on her hair and face through the small farmhouse windows. Pretty as a picture she was, and my, how she looked like she belonged there. William could only dream.

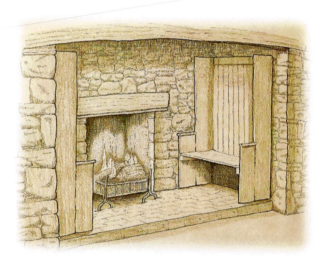

Young William was just twenty years of age when he stood once more by another burial in the farmyard plot. Old William Beer had been devastated by the loss of his lifetime partner, he only seemed to live on to complete his adopted son's education and to make arrangements for the farm. He died in his sleep, likely of a broken heart and yearning to be reunited with his dear Sarah. Farmer William Beer had been a well-liked member of the community, his trials and his forbearance appreciated by the good people of the moor. Many that attended the farm for his burial and wake, knew of the infant deaths he and his wife had endured and how they had come to adopt and love an orphan off the moors. The Richards family were there in strength, Hannah and her mother brought potato and bacon pies, and drink too for the celebration of old William's life, to remember him with fondness and to console and cheer young William, now all alone in the world. He would need more than confidence and great strength to survive life on the moors, as his dear father had discovered to his cost.

Taking a quiet moment away from the crowded farmhouse, William stood in silent thanks at the graveside for all he had received from the Beers, a decent life, the farm, a handful of sovereigns, the love of a family, nature's wisdom, the secrets of the moors. Slowly, someone came and stood respectfully close by. A kindly hand born of great strength touched his shoulder, it was Thomas Richards, 'sad day William, sad day. Now is your time to stand tall and honour their wish that you live on and do well. Be strong, remember them as they were in happy times. But you'll not do this on your own, not on the moors you won't. What you need is a good wife. Now I'm not sure if you have ever noticed her, but ever thought of asking my daughter Hannah? She's strong, thoughtful, loving, sews, cooks and can read and write by God. . . and she's pretty too!'

In his slumber, William relived the warmth of joyful remembrance of this conversation, turning ever hopefully to the smile, the hug, and the knowing look on Thomas' welcoming face. That afternoon William asked Hannah if she would consent to marry him. There was a short pause while she looked at the floor, then threw herself deeply into his arms. It must be said, there was a fair amount of cheering and back slapping at the farm that day. The Beer's faith in their boy was fully vindicated, life on the moors would continue.

Though still asleep by the fire, something in him sensed a powerful presence, something strongly akin to his own spirit was very close by.

Outside, the bewildered ghost of William's father watched snow falling upon the graves, just as it once had upon the living.

Inside, William was reliving the enduring memory of his final moments with his mother, he trembled as he felt the bitter cold of the east wind sleet in his face, remembered her shivering hands on his shoulders, the goodbye kiss on his forehead and her last words, never to give up.

Unexpectedly he realised he was awake and in his own home, he felt the warmth of the fire's embers, kindly hands on his shoulders and a warm, gentle and loving kiss on his forehead. He stood slowly, smiled, and embraced Hannah, forever the love of his life.

She smiled back at him, 'Time for bed William, it is late.'

KJH

Having sacrificed its own short life to keep at bay the
moorland darkness, the candle flame finally expired.
Moonlight, eternal mother of all hope, dutifully took
its place.
The sleeping farm dog rested peacefully, and the
glowing embers gently cooled to grey in the fire grate.
No more snow would fall that night,
just another storm, just another ending.

**

'Perhaps we could spare a moment
for all those brave souls, whoever and wherever they
are, that try as they might, can never make it home.
Thank you.'

Kelia-Jane Hannaford

We owe all we are -

to those who were.

KJH

**

About illustrator Kim Moody.

 Kim usually works with pen and ink, mainly on commissions for caricatures of houses for special gifts. His quirky line drawings appear as the successful 'Kim Moody' range of rubber art stamps, marketed by Chocolate Baroque Ltd.

Since 2009 he has edited the newsletter of BADFA, the British Association of Decorative and Folk Arts. He retired from 'real' work in 2017 and moved, with his wife, from the wilds of Hampshire to deepest, darkest Devon, England.

Visit his web site at :kpmoody.wordpress.com
Instagram   : kpm.illustration

Printed in Great Britain
by Amazon

81252543R00027